# Kalinka
## and
# Grakkle

for Eric Ernst Kaye

Published by
PEACHTREE PUBLISHERS
1700 Chattahoochee Avenue
Atlanta, Georgia 30318-2112
*www.peachtree-online.com*

Edited by Vicky Holifield
Design and composition by Nicola Simmonds Carmack

The illustrations were rendered in ink and gouache.

Printed in October 2017 by Tien Wah Press in Malaysia
10 9 8 7 6 5 4 3 2 1
First Edition
ISBN 978-1-68263-030-3

Library of Congress Cataloging-in-Publication Data

Names: Paschkis, Julie, author, illustrator.
Title: Kalinka and Grakkle / written and illustrated by Julie Paschkis.
Description: First edition. | Atlanta : Peachtree Publishers, [2018] | Summary: Kalinka, a little yellow bird who loves to be helpful, tries to tidy up the home of her grouchy neighbor, Grakkle, despite his protests.
Identifiers: LCCN 2017023979 | ISBN 9781682630303
Subjects: | CYAC: Helpfulness—Fiction. | Neighbors—Fiction. | Birds—Fiction. | Monsters—Fiction.
Classification: LCC PZ7.P2686 Kal 2018 | DDC [E]—dc23 LC record available at *https://lccn.loc.gov/2017023979*

# Kalinka
## and
# Grakkle

JULIE PASCHKIS

PEACHTREE
ATLANTA

Kalinka was a little yellow bird with a neat cap of red feathers.

"I'm such a good bird," she said to herself.

"Good as gold, with a cherry on top."

She lived next door to Grakkle. He was a burly beast with bad habits, a bad temper, and bad hair.

One day Kalinka flew through the open window of
Grakkle's house.

"Tsk-tsk!" she chirped. "This place could use some
tidying up."

"Grakk!" said Grakkle, stomping his foot. "Grakk! Grakk!"

"No bother at all," trilled Kalinka. "I'm a very good helper."

Grakkle didn't want any help.

He wanted some of his Auntie Grumble's homemade ginger cookies. He wanted to soak his tired, warty feet in a big bucket of pickle juice. But most of all he wanted to take a nap in his favorite comfortable chair.

Kalinka fluttered around and picked up the dirty socks scattered on the floor. She rolled some up and stuffed them in the woodstove. Then she hung some from the rafters.

"Gra-a-akk!" shouted Grakkle.

"You're welcome," said Kalinka.

Grakkle dumped his ginger cookies onto the table.

"Tsk-tsk!" cheeped Kalinka. "What a mess. I'll just put them on a plate for you...but maybe I should try one first."

She pecked at a cookie and it broke.

"Grakk!" screeched Grakkle.

"You're right," said Kalinka. "I'd better try another." And she did.

*Peck. Peck-peck. Peck-a-peck-peck.*

Soon nothing was left on the table but a pile of crumbs.

Grakkle swatted the little bird away and licked up what was left of his ginger cookies. "Gr-r-r-rakk," he growled.

"Don't mention it," said Kalinka.

Kalinka hopped to the counter. It was cluttered with letters and pencils and a crumpled-up brown bag.

"My feathers!" warbled Kalinka. "How untidy. Clearly my help is needed!"

In a flurry she flapped and flew around the room.

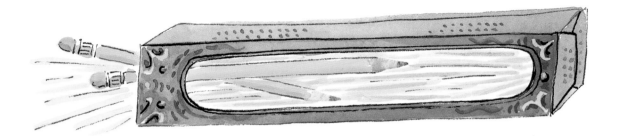

She poked the pencils into a box of spaghetti.

She carefully slid the mail into the toaster.

She put the bag on Grakkle's tail.

Grakkle swatted at the bag. He belched and scratched his head in confusion. His hair stood out every which way.

"This beast's appearance is appalling," said Kalinka. "Luckily for him, I do have a way with hair."

She perched on his head and got to work.

"Gr-r-r-r-rakk," grumbled Grakkle.

"You're welcome," said Kalinka, tying a bow in his matted hair.

Kalinka fluffed her feathers and yawned. "I'm worn out from being such a good helper."

She flew straight to Grakkle's favorite comfortable chair.

In fact, it was his *only* comfortable chair.

She settled down in the middle of the soft round cushion and closed her eyes.

"Grakk! Grakk! Grakk!" yelled Grakkle.

"What a lovely lullaby," said Kalinka. "Thank you."

"Gr-r-r-r-rakk," groaned Grakkle.

The burly beast swished his tail.

He stomped and snarled and waved his arms.

Kalinka sighed in her sleep.

Grakkle began to throw things—

The crumpled-up paper bag.

A pencil.

An apple.

And finally he hurled his Auntie Grumble's cookbook…
which hit the table and skidded into the back of the chair…
which teetered and tottered
until Kalinka toppled off the soft round cushion
and fell…

PLOP!

right

into

the pickle bucket

where Grakkle

soaked his warty feet.


Kalinka thrashed.

She flapped her wings in the greenish brine.

Then she sputtered

and

sank.

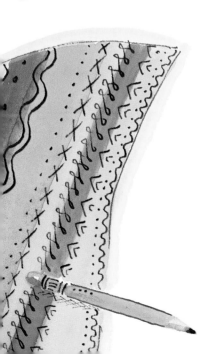

Grakkle gasped. "Grakk?"

What had he done?

He rushed over and turned the bucket upside down.

*Splash!*

Grakkle scooped Kalinka into his paws.

He patted her dry with the tip of his tail.

He hugged her tightly with his hairy arms.

He blew on her feathers with his hot breath.

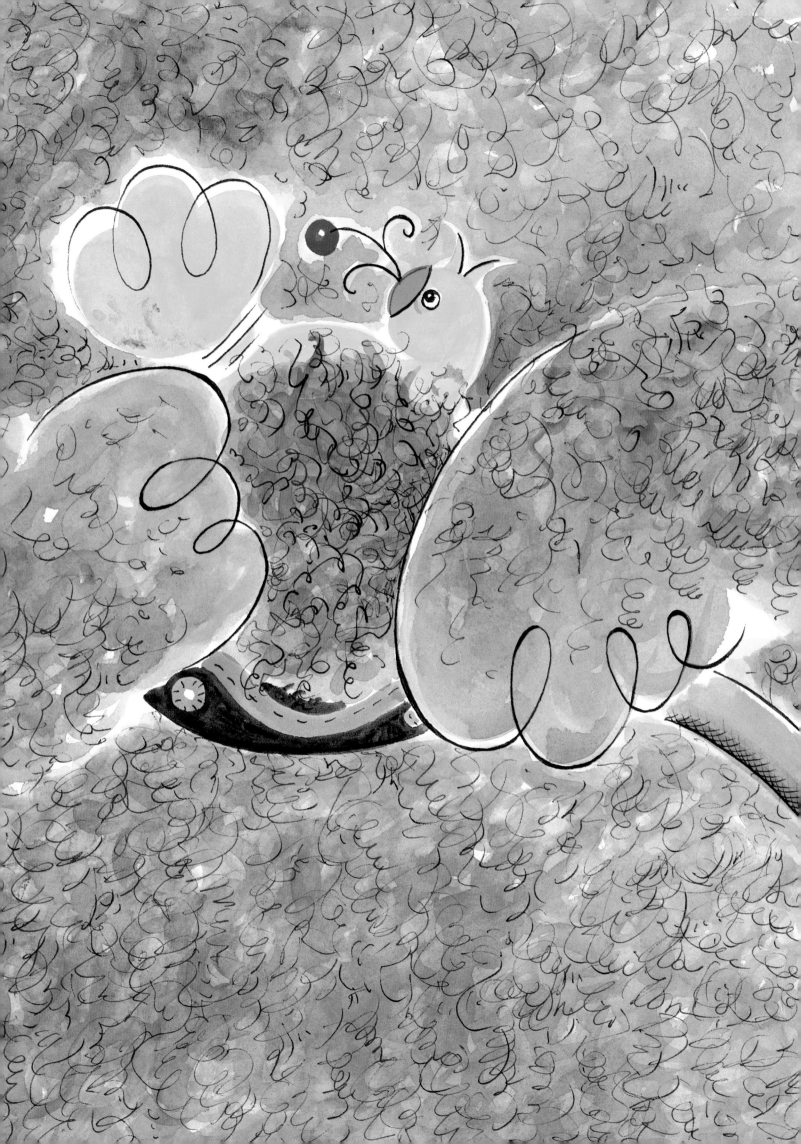

Kalinka coughed. "Gra-a-a-ak!" she croaked.

"You're welcome," said Grakkle.

He looked at her.

She looked at him.

Then they both cracked up.

"Grakk, grakk!"

"Grak-grak-grak!"

Grakkle yawned and looked at the topsy-turvy room. He picked up his favorite comfortable chair and plopped down on the soft round cushion.

Kalinka yawned, too. She made a little nest in Grakkle's tangled hair, fluffed up her feathers, and snuggled in.

Together they took a long afternoon nap.

Together they gently snored.

*G-rrr-a-a-akk, g-rrr-a-a-akk, g-rrr-a-a-akk…*